# Mike Boldt

# COLORS

*versus*

SHAPES

HARPER
*An Imprint of HarperCollinsPublishers*

ISBN 978-0-06-210303-1 (trade bdg.)

The artist used Corel Painter to digitally create the illustrations for this book.
Typography by Dana Fritts
14 15 16 17 18   SCP   10 9 8 7 6 5 4 3 2 1
❖ First Edition

For
Eli, Naomi
& Alyse

You
Rock.

3 6109 00461 4399

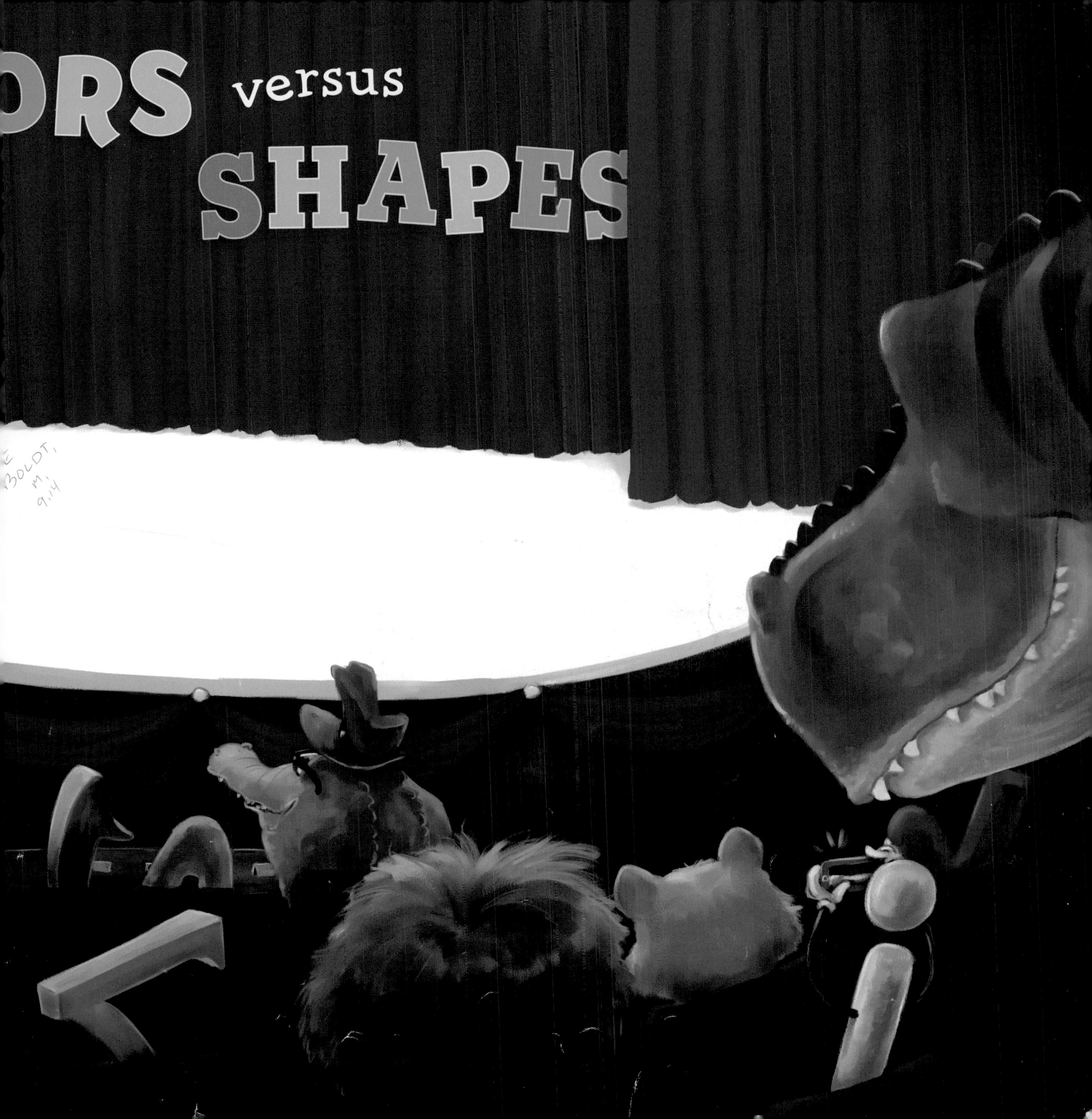
ORS versus
SHAPES

Hardly. Gaze upon some real talent as these two **triangles** trampoline right into a **square!**

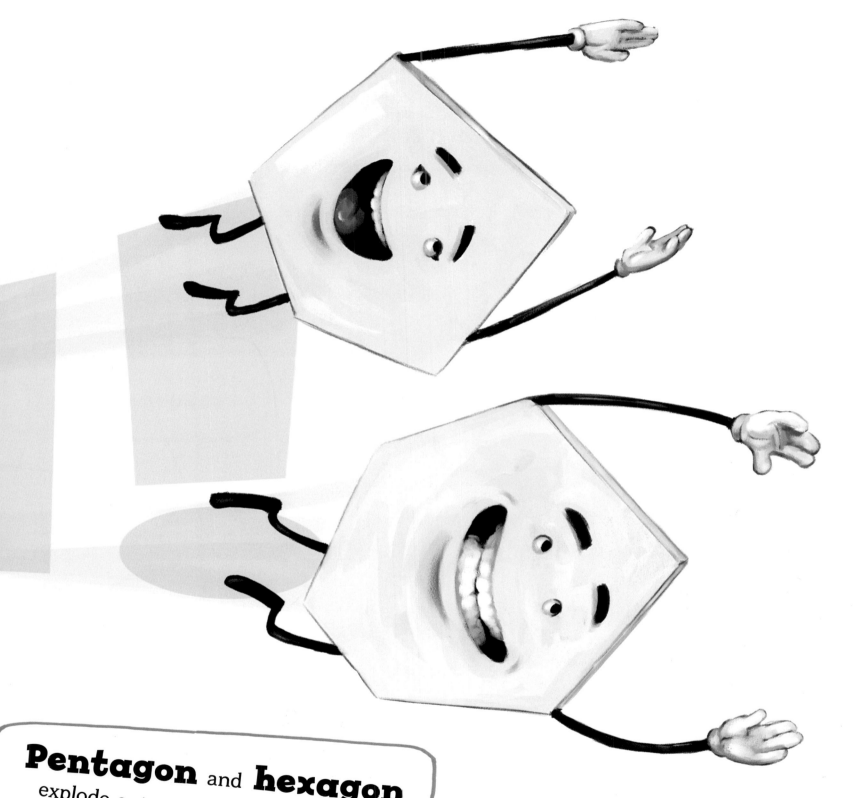

**Pentagon** and **hexagon**
explode onto the scene.

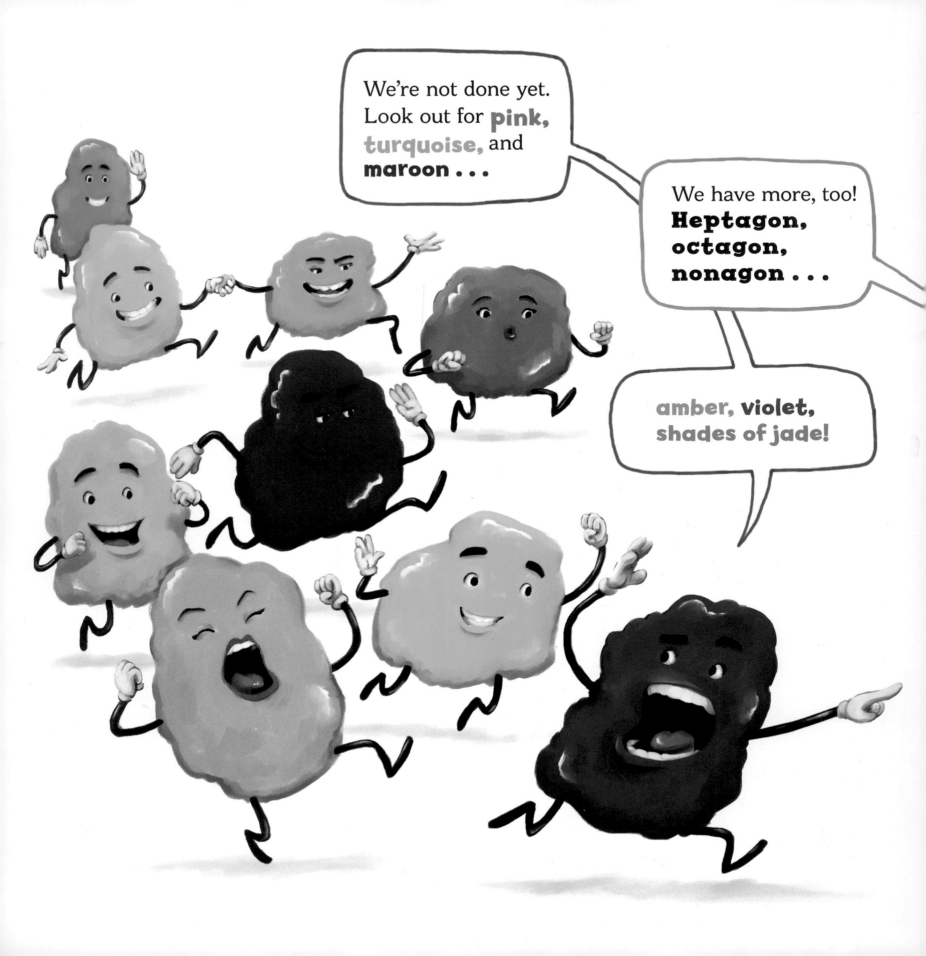